Cup
Doesn't Flip
Hamburgers

There are more books about the Bailey School Kids!
Have you read these adventures?

Vampires Don't Wear Polka Dots
Leprechauns Don't Play Basketball
Santa Claus Doesn't Mop Floors
Werewolves Don't Go to Summer Camp
Ghosts Don't Eat Potato Chips
Frankenstein Doesn't Plant Petunias
Aliens Don't Wear Braces
Genies Don't Ride Bicycles
Pirates Don't Wear Pink Sunglasses
Witches Don't Do Backflips
Skeletons Don't Play Tubas

Flip
Hamburgers

by Debbie Dadey
and
Marcia Thornton Jones

Illustrated by John Steven Gurney

A
LITTLE APPLE
PAPERBACK

SCHOLASTIC INC.
New York   Toronto   London   Auckland   Sydney

To our special valentines: Steve and Eric
— MTJ and DD

ISBN 0-590-48114-2

Text copyright © 1995 by Debbie S. Dadey and Marcia Thorton Jones
Illustrations copyright © 1995 by Scholastic Inc.
All rights reserved. Published by Scholastic Inc.
APPLE PAPERBACKS is a registered trademark of Scholastic Inc.

48 47 46   15 16/0

Printed in the U.S.A.   40

First Scholastic printing, January 1995

Book design by Laurie Williams

1

St. Valentine's Day

"Pink lace and frills! This is girls' stuff," Eddie complained, crumpling the paper valentine he was making into a wad. He glanced around the classroom to make sure his teacher, Mrs. Jeepers, wasn't watching. After all, most kids thought she was a vampire, and didn't dare do anything to make her green eyes flash.

Luckily for Eddie, Mrs. Jeepers was busy at the door talking to Principal Davis. Eddie eyed his target. A head full of bouncy yellow curls was just three seats away. With careful aim, he let his ruined valentine soar across the aisle. *Smack!* It landed right in the middle of Carey's blonde head.

"Bingo!" Eddie mouthed when Carey

twisted around to give him a mean look.

"I bet you won't get a single valentine," Carey blurted out. Unfortunately, she was so mad, she forgot to whisper. The class gasped when Mrs. Jeepers slowly turned around and flashed her eyes at Carey.

"I am surprised to hear such a terrible insult," Mrs. Jeepers said in her strange Transylvanian accent.

"But, Eddie threw — " Carey started to say.

"Enough!" Mrs. Jeepers interrupted and rubbed her green brooch. "Valentine's Day is a time to show people we appreciate them. You must apologize for being rude."

Carey's face turned bright red. "But . . ."

"Apologize," Mrs. Jeepers insisted.

The rest of the class watched as Carey faced Eddie. "I'm sorry," she muttered through clenched teeth. Then she turned around and stared at the half-made valentine on her own desk.

Eddie smiled his sweetest smile until Mrs. Jeepers went back to talking with Principal Davis. Then he giggled as he pulled the eraser off his pencil and flicked it.

Carey flinched when the eraser popped her on the back. But she wasn't about to turn around and get in trouble again, and Eddie knew it.

Melody sat behind Eddie. "You'd better stop it," she warned. "Before Mrs. Jeepers catches you."

But Eddie was having too much fun. As long as Mrs. Jeepers was busy, he was going to keep it up. He was just about to send a broken crayon hurtling toward Carey when Mrs. Jeepers looked at the class and cleared her throat. Eddie quickly sat up straight and smiled sweetly.

"It is time for us to go to the cafeteria,"

Mrs. Jeepers said. Then she smiled an odd little half-smile. "Today, we will meet our new cook, Mrs. Rosenbloom."

Half the class groaned, but Liza raised her hand. "Maybe we should give Mrs. Rosenbloom a valentine, too."

"What a wonderful idea," Mrs. Jeepers said. "Please line up and bring one of your cards." Most of the kids rushed to line up, but Eddie, Liza, Melody, and Howie waited to be last.

"That was a dopey idea," Eddie told Liza.

"You're just mad because you didn't get any valentine cards made," Howie interrupted.

Melody nodded. "You were too busy bothering Carey."

"And she's never going to forgive you," Liza added. "Carey has never been in trouble before."

"I don't care about her or valentines," Eddie said, shaking his head as they headed for the lunchroom. "But I do care about my empty stomach. I'm hungry. We always have the same old slop in the cafeteria."

"Maybe the new cook will be different," Liza said.

Eddie shook his head. "That just means we'll have new slop."

"Eddie, you should give her a chance. She may be a really good cook," Melody said as they walked into the cafeteria.

"It'll be the first good cook at Ba — " Eddie said, but he stopped at the entrance of the cafeteria.

"What in the world happened?" Howie asked.

2

Explosion

"It looks like a card store exploded in here," Howie said, looking around the cafeteria. All sizes of red, pink, and white paper hearts were everywhere the kids looked. Hearts were plastered to the walls, hanging from the ceiling, and even stuck onto the garbage cans.

Melody giggled. "They must have had a five-for-one heart sale."

"Five dumb decorations for the price of one," Eddie said. "This place looks stupid."

"I think it's pretty," Liza said. "After all, Valentine's Day is less than a week away."

Eddie rolled his eyes. "Valentine's Day is for three year olds who don't have anything better to do."

"Valentine's Day is for telling people you like them," Melody told him.

"Or that you love them," Liza giggled.

"That's disgusting," Eddie said.

"There's nothing disgusting about *love*," said a voice from beside them. "But you'll find that out soon enough."

Eddie looked up and gulped. In front of him was the biggest red dress he'd ever seen and it was being worn by the biggest woman he'd ever seen. Almost everything about her was big and red, from her big, bright red lips to her fluffy reddish-blonde hair. Even the heart button on her apron and her dangling heart earrings were big and red.

But when she grabbed Eddie's cheeks, he noticed that her fingernails were painted hot pink with little white arrows on them. "You're just the cutest little thing," the woman said as she squeezed Eddie's cheeks. "I just *love* your red hair. What a cutie pie!"

"You must be Mrs. Rosenbloom, the new cook," Liza said. "Welcome to Bailey Elementary." Liza held out her valentine to the big woman.

"Why, thank you, sugar." Mrs. Rosenbloom smiled and gave Liza a bear hug. "I just know I'm going to *love* it here!"

"We hope so," Howie said politely. "Did you do the decorating?"

"Why, yes." Mrs. Rosenbloom blushed. "I just *love* Valentine's Day. But that's enough talking. Come eat."

The four kids followed the rest of their class through the lunch line and picked up their trays.

"I've never seen so much red in my life," Eddie said. Everything on their lunch trays was red. There was heart-shaped meatloaf covered with ketchup and a tomato slice in a heart shape. Each tray had a slice of red apple with a heart-shaped blob of cherry Jell-O. There were even red straws for the milk.

"I think this lady fell off the old holiday wagon before her brain was fully cooked," Eddie said when they sat down with their trays. "She's gone heart crazy."

"I think it's nice," Liza said. "It sure beats the tuna surprise we usually have on Mondays."

"Baked bowling balls would beat that," Melody agreed after taking a bite of the Jell-O. "This stuff may be red, but it's good."

"There's nothing good about overdosing on red," Eddie said. "That new cook may need surgery to remove all these hearts. And I'm just the doctor to handle it."

"Who are you?" Howie laughed. "Doctor Love?"

"Doctor Meanie would be more like it," Liza said. "Don't go bothering Mrs. Rosenbloom. She's nice."

Eddie smiled. "Would I bother a sweet lady like her?"

His three friends all nodded their heads yes. Eddie had a reputation for causing mischief. But none of the four kids noticed Mrs. Rosenbloom standing nearby. She was touching her heart button and she was smiling.

3

Love Bug

"There's that prissy Carey kissing up to Mrs. Rosenbloom," Eddie pointed as he slurped the last of his cherry Jell-O.

"No fair!" Melody said. "Mrs. Rosenbloom is giving Carey a heart button and a cookie."

"Carey gets everything." Liza sighed. Carey's dad owned the Bailey City Bank. Carey was always bringing new toys to school or bragging about something her dad bought her.

"I'll make sure she gets a hard time," Eddie said with an evil grin. He grabbed his half-empty lunch tray and headed for Carey. Mrs. Rosenbloom finished pinning the button on Carey and spun her around to face Eddie.

"Why, hello, Eddie," Carey said with a

13

mouth full of cookie. "Fancy meeting you here."

"Yeah, it's a miracle," Eddie said. "Would you like my apple slice?"

"I'd *love* it!" Carey said, snapping it off Eddie's tray. "But, then, I'd adore anything of yours!" She batted her eyelashes at Eddie before nibbling on the apple. Eddie gave her a funny look, then rushed back to his seat.

"I can't believe you gave Carey your apple," Melody said. "I thought you hated her."

"I can't stand her," Eddie agreed. "I dropped it on the floor. That's why I gave it to her."

"That wasn't very nice," Liza said.

"Speaking of nice. Do you see the way Carey keeps looking at you?" Howie asked Eddie. The four kids turned to see Carey tossing her blonde hair and fluttering her eyebrows in their direction.

Melody giggled. "I think she's been bitten by the love bug!"

"You guys are crazy." Eddie shook his head and looked at Carey. She smiled and blew him a kiss!

Eddie splashed through a mud puddle on his way across the playground the next morning. Melody, Liza, and Howie were huddled under a huge oak tree comparing answers to their math homework.

"Number thirteen has to be three hundred and forty-two hearts," Melody was explaining.

Howie shook his head. "You weren't supposed to add. You should have subtracted."

Liza frowned. "I multiplied! What did you get for the answer, Eddie?"

Eddie looked at his friends like they'd just sprouted broccoli out of their ears. "What homework?"

Melody rolled her eyes. "You'll never make it out of third grade unless you do the homework."

"I'll help you," a sweet voice interrupted.

The four friends turned to face Carey. She winked at Eddie. "I have all the answers and mine are always right."

Eddie kicked his foot into the mud, splattering Carey's pink boots with brown goo. "I don't need any help," he said, "especially from you." Then he stomped toward the school.

"But I don't mind helping *you*," Carey insisted as she grabbed his elbow. "I brought you something, too."

Eddie skidded to a stop. "You're trying to get me back for yesterday's paper wad. You'd give me the wrong answers just to get me in trouble."

"Don't be silly," Carey said, batting her eyelashes at him. "Here, this proves I'm not mad at you." She reached inside her bookbag and pulled out a red rose. "I even snipped the thorns off so you won't get pricked."

Eddie backed away and bumped into Melody.

"It's not every day a guy gets a flower from his girlfriend," Melody said with a giggle.

"Carey is not my girlfriend!" Eddie yelled as he ran into the school.

Carey sighed and flipped her golden curls behind her ears. "Poor Eddie. I'll just have to try harder."

"Try harder to do what?" Liza asked from behind Melody.

Carey looked at Melody, Howie, and Liza as if she were going to tell them the answers to next week's science test. But then she shook her head and followed Eddie into the school. "Never mind. You just wouldn't understand."

"Something strange is going on at Bailey Elementary," Melody said.

Howie nodded. "I never dreamed I'd see the day when Carey was nice to Eddie."

"It's almost like she's in love with him," Liza said softly.

"Don't be silly," Melody said. "Godzilla is more lovable than Eddie." The three friends nodded and went inside the school building. Once inside, the kids stopped dead in their tracks.

"Maybe Liza's right," Howie said.

Melody started laughing so hard, she snorted through her nose. "It looks like Carey has Eddie cornered."

Sure enough, Carey had grabbed Eddie's notebook at the water fountain. "I'd *love* to carry your books," she was telling him.

Eddie tugged as hard as he could, but Carey wouldn't let go. "Give it to me!" Eddie jerked his notebook one last time, tearing the cover in half. "Now look what you've done!" Eddie yelled.

"I'm sorry," Carey said. "I'll get you a new one."

Eddie gave her a look and dashed into the classroom. Melody, Howie, and Liza followed and started teasing Eddie.

"It looks like Carey's fallen for you," Howie whispered.

Eddie took a pencil out of his desk and shook his head. "She's just trying to make me mad."

"It looks like love to me." Melody nodded toward the doorway. Carey stood there straightening the heart pin on her pink sweater. Then she strode to Eddie and paused beside his desk. She smiled and put a chocolate kiss on his desk. She winked and walked to her own desk.

From behind him, Eddie heard Melody giggle as she started singing. "Eddie and Carey, sitting in a tree, K-I-S-S-I-N-G . . . first comes love . . ."

But before she could sing any more, Eddie took the candy kiss and flung it over his shoulder. It landed with a definite *thunk* on Melody's forehead.

4

Lovesick

For the first time in his life, Eddie kept his eyes on his schoolwork. He didn't actually do much of it, but he kept his eyes on his paper anyway. He didn't want to look up and catch Carey staring at him again. That's what had happened right in the middle of the science experiment. She'd smiled and winked at him. Then she blew him a kiss. Eddie had spilled an entire test tube of saltwater in his lap.

Then Howie made kissing noises. "Quit it," Eddie warned. "Or I'll smack you right across the face."

By lunchtime, Eddie was ready to leave school and Bailey City, too. Melody grabbed his shoulder. "Looks like you've

22

fallen in love with the smartest girl in class," she teased.

"She must not be that smart," Howie interrupted. "Not if she likes Eddie!"

"That's enough," Eddie sputtered. "There is something very fishy about this."

"I'll say." Melody laughed. "It's fishy that anyone would bring you red roses and candy kisses."

Liza nodded. "All you deserve are thorns and spinach."

Eddie turned his back on his friends and hurried to lunch. The whole school had turned against him. Everyone that is, except Carey. And that was even worse.

Red and pink hearts were still all over the cafeteria. Eddie had already had his fill of Valentine's Day nonsense. He grabbed his tray of a heart-shaped sandwich, a pink-frosted cupcake, and cherry-flavored juice and headed for the corner table. He didn't speak when Liza, Howie, and Melody sat down. Instead, he

kept his eyes on the new cook. There was something about her that bothered him.

He watched her smile and hand out trays of pink and red goop. But Eddie stopped chewing his heart-shaped sandwich when Ben came through the line. Ben was the biggest bully in the fourth grade. Eddie got some of his best ideas from watching Ben. Eddie couldn't wait to see how Ben handled the new cook.

"Why so grumpy?" Mrs. Rosenbloom put her hands on her wide waist and laughed. "You need something to sweeten up your insides." Then she pulled a huge cookie from off a top shelf. It was smothered in icing and little pieces of red candy. Eddie licked his lips as Ben wolfed down the cookie.

With his hands full, Ben couldn't stop Mrs. Rosenbloom from pinning a heart button onto his shirt. "That ought to do the trick," Mrs. Rosenbloom said as Ben walked away still chomping on the cookie.

Eddie's eyes widened when he saw the button. It was identical to Carey's.

Eddie smiled when Ben stopped beside Isabell Hart. "Look," Eddie said to his friends. "Ben's going to let prissy Issy have it."

The four kids watched. But Ben didn't spit or burp or tease Issy. Instead, he sat down beside her and shared his cookie.

Eddie drummed his fingers on the table. Something was wrong, really wrong, but he couldn't put his finger on it. And then it came to him. He slapped the table with his hand, sending spoons and forks clattering to the floor. "I've got it!" he blurted.

"Got what?" Melody asked. "The chicken pox?"

Eddie ignored Melody. "I've got the answer to everything."

"Great," Howie said. "Then you can take my science test for me."

"No," Eddie snapped. "I know why Carey and Ben are acting like lovesick slugs."

"Why?" Liza asked.

Eddie looked at his friends and kept his voice low. "Everything was normal until yesterday."

"Nothing is ever normal at Bailey Elementary," Melody interrupted.

Eddie nodded. "But until then, Carey

and Ben were the same old pests."

"What are you getting at?" Howie asked.

"It's the work of Mrs. Rosenbloom," Eddie explained. "She's invaded Bailey Elementary and she's armed with love potions!"

5

Love Potions

Howie choked on his heart-shaped sandwich and Melody laughed so hard, she spit milk onto the table. Even Liza got caught in a fit of giggles.

"There are no such things as love potions," Melody told Eddie while she mopped up her milk using a red heart napkin.

"Mrs. Rosenbloom is just spreading good cheer," Liza said. "There's nothing wrong with being nice."

"There is if you don't want to be nice," Eddie snapped. "Mrs. Rosenbloom is ruining Bailey Elementary. Everyone is turning into gushy, oogle-eyed love-struck twirps!"

"You make Mrs. Rosenbloom sound like Cupid," Melody said.

"Who?" Eddie and Liza asked together.

Howie pointed to a picture on the wall. "Cupid is the fat little baby who shoots arrows at people. Whoever gets hit with an arrow falls in love."

Eddie shrugged. "Who knows? Maybe she is Cupid. She's not a baby, but you have to admit, she is pretty chubby."

His three friends started laughing again. Eddie glared at them and stood up to leave. "You wait and see. Before long, everyone will be a lovey-dovey goodie two-shoes and it'll all be Mrs. Rosenbloom's fault!" Eddie left his giggling friends and threw his trash in the garbage can. When he turned to leave, his view was blocked by a huge red wall with lacy pockets. He slowly looked up, right into the grinning face of Mrs. Rosenbloom.

"Howdy," Mrs. Rosenbloom said. "It looks like you've lost your best friend. I bet a big old sugar cookie would fill your day with sunshine."

"N-n-no thanks," Eddie stuttered and backed away. He bumped right into Carey.

Carey smiled and batted her eyelashes at Eddie. "How about a chocolate kiss?" she asked.

Eddie looked at Mrs. Rosenbloom and at Carey. Then he did the only thing he could do. He ran. He darted past a very surprised Mrs. Rosenbloom. He skidded around a corner and raced back to the classroom as fast as he could.

Eddie's heart was still thumping when the rest of the class quietly filed into the third-grade room.

Melody whispered to Eddie, "Mrs. Jeepers will turn you into bat bait when she finds out you were running in the cafeteria."

Howie nodded. "I bet Mrs. Rosenbloom is telling her how rude you were."

"I wasn't being rude," Eddie argued. "I was running for my life."

Liza laughed. "You were running from a sugar cookie."

"A cookie filled with love potion," Eddie said.

"You're going to need some of that love potion to save you from Mrs. Jeepers," Melody warned. Their teacher didn't allow her students to be rude. The kids got quiet as Mrs. Jeepers came into the room and looked at Eddie.

But Mrs. Jeepers didn't flash her eyes at Eddie and she didn't rub her mysterious brooch like she usually did when she was angry. Instead, she smiled. Her cheeks were flushed rosy-red, instead of their usual chalk-white color.

"What's wrong with her?" Liza whispered. "Do you think she's sick?"

No one had time to answer, because a loud knock at the door interrupted them. Principal Davis opened the door, wearing a huge heart pin. He held out a sugar cookie and smiled at Mrs. Jeepers. "You forgot your cookie," he said. "So I brought it to you."

Mrs. Jeepers' face blushed to a deep shade of purple. She took the half-eaten cookie from Principal Davis. "Why, thank you," she said. "I do *love* sugar cookies."

Principal Davis smiled and waved good-bye. "I was happy to bring it."

Mrs. Jeepers closed the door and faced her class. What Eddie saw made him drop his math book. Mrs. Jeepers was wearing a heart pin, too.

6

Button Attack

"Don't you guys get it?" Eddie yelled. "She's taking over our school!"

"Eddie, you have the craziest imagination," Liza told him. Liza, Melody, Eddie, and Howie were all gathered under their favorite oak tree after school.

Melody agreed. "I've heard people say that love is war — "

"It's the attack of the killer buttons!" Eddie interrupted. "Everybody who wears one and eats a sugar cookie goes love crazy!"

"That's ridiculous!" Liza said. "Just because Mrs. Jeepers is wearing a heart button is nothing to get excited about. After all, she wears a green brooch every day."

"But it's not every day that she acts like

a lovesick puppy," Eddie pointed out.

Howie leaned against the oak tree. "She did act stranger than usual. At recess time, she actually was humming a song."

"It was a love song," Melody said. "And during math, she drew hearts on the board! She's never done that before."

"See!" Eddie yelled. "I told you something like this was going to happen, but you wouldn't believe me. We have to do something before it's too late."

"Hold on just a minute," Melody said. "There's nothing wrong with drawing hearts or humming love songs. The world would probably be a lot better if everyone was a little more loving."

"Melody is right. Just think what it would be like if everyone loved everyone else," Liza said.

Eddie started to say something, but he didn't get the chance. Carey came up behind him and put her hands over his eyes.

"Guess who?" Carey said.

"My worst nightmare!" Eddie yelled and pushed Carey's hands away.

Carey winked and grabbed Eddie's hand. "Oh, Eddie. You are so funny. Would you like to walk me home?"

"No!" Eddie hollered and pulled away. "No! No!" Eddie looked at Howie, Liza, and Melody. "See! Just look what that cook has done. She's taken two perfectly good enemies and spoiled them."

Carey batted her eyelashes at Eddie. "We could never be enemies. I like you too much. As a matter of fact, I lo — "

"Aaahhh!" Eddie screamed. "This has gone too far! I've got to do something!" Then he ran out of the playground and didn't stop until he was safe at home.

Carey looked at Melody, Howie, and Liza. "He's playing hard to get," Carey said. "I think I'll bake him some sugar cookies."

The next morning, Eddie came to school and didn't say a word. He didn't say anything when Howie said hello, and he just put his head down when Carey offered him a big fat red cookie and gave him a new pink notebook. He didn't even comment when Mrs. Jeepers came in wearing a bright red dress with a white rose in her hair.

"I saw Principal Davis give her that rose," Liza whispered. "I think they're in love. Mrs. Jeepers has probably been lonely since her husband died."

"Maybe you were right about those buttons and cookies," Howie muttered. Eddie didn't say a word, but he did notice that Mrs. Jeepers was still wearing her heart button.

Finally at lunch, Eddie spoke. "Whatever happens, don't eat one of those heart cookies or wear one of those buttons."

Liza rolled her eyes. "You still don't believe that Cupid nonsense, do you? Just look at Mrs. Rosenbloom. She looks perfectly innocent."

The four friends looked through the open kitchen door. Mrs. Rosenbloom was there in a bright red dress with a white apron and a big white hat. She was busy cooking heart-shaped hamburgers on the grill. Every once in a while, she would toss one of the burgers. The hamburger

would swirl through the air and Mrs. Rosenbloom would catch it on a plate.

"I've never seen Cupid flipping hamburgers before," Melody said.

"Maybe she's the first one," Eddie said. "After all, Cupids have to eat, too. That's how they get so fat."

"You're crazy," Liza said. "Besides, those cookies that she baked look good. Just look at those yummy red sprinkles on top. I have to get one." Liza stood up to go into the kitchen and Melody followed.

"I'm going to get one of those cute buttons," Melody added.

Eddie shook his head at Howie and took a bite of his heart-shaped hamburger. "Somebody has to cure Bailey School kids of this lovesickness. And it will have to be me."

7

Love Is War

Melody closed her eyes and swallowed. "This is the best cookie I've ever sunk my teeth into."

Liza nodded and licked a few sprinkles off her red cookie. "I just *love* them!"

Melody giggled, and she and Liza walked back toward their seats in the lunchroom. "But nothing is sweeter than Howie. He's so cute and smart."

"I'm glad he's my friend," Liza told her. "I think he likes me better than you."

"Your brain is as mushy as oatmeal," Melody snapped. "Howie likes me best."

Liza sniffed and touched Melody's arm. "He does not."

"Does too!" Melody pushed her best friend.

Liza fell against the wall and slid to the

floor. "Look what you did!" Liza shrieked.

"It's your own fault," Melody yelled. The rest of the kids in the cafeteria fell silent. Melody and Liza had been best friends since kindergarten. They hardly ever had fights.

Howie and Eddie stared at Liza and Melody. "What's gotten into them?" Eddie asked.

Howie shrugged. "We'd better help them out. If Mrs. Jeepers finds out they were fighting, she'll send them to Principal Davis' office."

Howie and Eddie rushed across the crowded cafeteria. Without thinking, Howie held out his hand to help Liza up.

Liza smiled sweetly and batted her eyelashes. Then she gently placed her hand in Howie's. "See," she told Melody. "Howie likes me best."

Howie's mouth dropped open and his face turned as red as the sprinkles on

Mrs. Rosenbloom's cookies. "I never said that!" Howie sputtered.

Liza squeezed his hand and winked. "It's okay, Howie. I like you, too!"

Howie pulled his hand away and took three steps back. "What's wrong with you, Liza?" he asked. "Are you sick?"

Eddie stepped between Liza and Howie. "Liza's sick, all right. Lovesick."

"Am not!" Liza blurted. "Melody's the one who's sick. She thinks Howie likes her better than me! Tell her the truth, Howie!"

Howie looked at Liza, then at Melody. If he said he liked Liza, Melody would get mad. If he said he liked Melody, Liza would get upset and her nose would bleed. "I like you both," he finally admitted. "We're friends."

"You can't like us both," Melody snapped. "You have to pick who you like best." She put her hands on her hips and waited.

Eddie grabbed Howie's elbow and pulled him away. "Don't say a word," he warned. "Thanks to Mrs. Rosenbloom's love potion, Bailey Elementary is on the brink of war!"

8

Cupid's Cure

"Here comes Carey," Howie warned Eddie. The two boys had fled the cafeteria and were sneaking to their classroom. They ducked into the gym before Carey spotted them.

"Now do you believe Mrs. Rosenbloom is Cupid?" Eddie asked. "And that she invaded Bailey Elementary armed with love potion cookies?"

Howie didn't want to admit that Eddie was right, but he was still shaking from Liza and Melody's fight. "But where are Cupid's arrows?"

"I figured it out," Eddie said. "Instead of shooting people with arrows, Mrs. Rosenbloom is sticking them with those silly heart buttons. She only gives them to victims who eat one of her special

cookies. All we have to do is stay away from people with those buttons."

"We can't run from everyone with those buttons for the rest of our lives," Howie said.

"Of course not," Eddie told him. "Just until school is over today."

"Then what will we do?" Howie asked. "Carey is hunting you down like a cat hunts mice, and I'm about to lose two friends. And if Mrs. Jeepers gets her fangs into Principal Davis, we'll really be doomed. Can you imagine Dracula for a principal? We have to figure something out soon."

"We'll go to my house after school to work on a cure for Mrs. Rosenbloom's love disease," Eddie decided.

Howie moaned and checked to see if Carey was gone. "What will we do if the cure doesn't work?"

"It has to work," Eddie said slowly. "Our happiness depends on it!"

For the rest of the day, Howie and Eddie avoided anyone wearing heart buttons. It wasn't easy to do. It seemed like half the school was wearing them.

During social studies, Carey tried to pass Eddie a love note, but Eddie just knocked it on the floor. Liza and Melody snapped at each other during science and Howie thought they were going to start fighting.

As soon as school was dismissed, Howie

and Eddie scooted out the door and raced down Delaware Boulevard toward Eddie's house.

Eddie's grandmother was in the kitchen. She was famous for her creative casseroles, and she liked to whip up things using unusual ingredients. She looked at Eddie and Howie when they slammed the back door.

"Grandma!" Eddie panted. "You've got to help us!"

Eddie's grandmother tapped the spoon on the side of the bowl. "What's wrong? Are you in trouble again?"

"Big trouble," Eddie admitted. "But this time it's not my fault."

"That's the truth," Howie added. "It's Liza, and Melody, and Carey, and — "

"Slow down," Eddie's grandmother interrupted and showed the boys a heaping plate of sugar cookies. "Have a snack and then we'll talk about this horrible girl problem."

Eddie's face turned the color of milk and Howie held up his hands. "No way!" Eddie snapped. "We've had enough cookies to last a lifetime."

"Well, I'm glad to hear that." Eddie's grandmother laughed. "I guess what they say is true."

"What's true?" Howie asked.

"That rhyme about girls and boys," Eddie's grandmother said matter-of-factly. "Sugar and spice and everything nice — "

"That's it!" Eddie yelped before his grandmother could finish. "I've got the answer."

9

Pucker Power

"Can Howie and I use the kitchen to make something?" Eddie asked his grandmother.

"You're not going to make a bomb or poison, are you?" his grandmother asked.

"No." Eddie shook his head. "Just some cookie dough."

"All right," she said. "But don't make a mess."

Eddie's grandmother wiped her hands on a kitchen towel and went into the laundry room. Before long, the boys heard her humming as she ironed clothes.

"What does sugar and spice have to do with a cure for Mrs. Rosenbloom's love potion?" Howie asked.

"Grandma says that rhyme all the time. It's: *Sugar and spice and everything nice, that's what little girls are made of. Snips and snails and puppy dog tails, that's what little boys are made of.*"

"So?" Howie said, scratching his head.

"So, what's the opposite of sweet sugar?" Eddie asked.

Howie looked at Eddie and thought. "Sour puppy dog tails," he said finally.

"Exactly," Eddie said, slapping Howie on the back. "That's the cure."

"Puppy dog tails?" Howie yelled. "I'm not making anything with dog tails in it."

Eddie shook his head. "We don't need dogs. We're going to make something so sour that love will be the last thing anyone thinks about when they eat it." Eddie pulled jars out of the refrigerator and cabinets along with a big bowl and spoon.

"If it tastes that bad, no one is going to eat it," Howie said.

"You just help me make it," Eddie explained. "I'll take care of getting them to eat it."

Howie shrugged his shoulders and reached for a bottle. It was vinegar. He poured half the bottle into Eddie's big bowl. "Vinegar is disgusting. I tasted it one time," Howie said.

"That's the spirit. That'll give it pucker power," Eddie said. "Let's start mixing." Howie stirred the ingredients while Eddie dumped in one thing after another. He added lemon juice, garlic powder, and black pepper.

"It's too runny," Howie said. "We need something to make it stick together."

Eddie nodded and looked inside the refrigerator. He pulled out the mustard. After emptying half the jar into the bowl, Eddie said, "That looks like cookie dough to me. We can add it to Mrs. Rosenbloom's batter and she will never know the difference."

"No, she'll know. This stuff is bright yellow and her cookies are red. This

would make them turn orange," Howie said.

"I can fix that," Eddie said. He whipped a big container out of the refrigerator and squeezed it. The bowl quickly filled with bright red ketchup. Howie stirred and stirred until the mixture was solid red.

Howie and Eddie looked in the bowl and smiled. "Perfect," they said together.

10

Hand in the Cookie Jar

Before school the next morning, Eddie and Howie met under the big oak tree. "Did you bring it?" Howie asked.

"Yeah," Eddie said, patting his backpack. "I had to tell Grandma it was a science project to get it out of the house."

"It *is* an experiment," Howie said. "I just hope it works." The two boys quietly walked into the building and straight to the lunchroom.

"Mrs. Rosenbloom's in there," Eddie hissed as they peeked into the kitchen. The two boys saw the red-dressed cook sitting at a counter making heart-shaped sandwiches. Behind her was a big bowl of cookie dough.

As the boys were watching, Mrs. Rosenbloom started singing, very loudly and off-key. "I *love* Valentine's Day . . ."

Eddie giggled. "I wish she'd quit that racket. She's hurting my ears."

"My *love* is higher than the highest mountain!" Mrs. Rosenbloom bellowed as she added cheese to the sandwiches.

"She belongs high on a mountain," Eddie said, "like way in the clouds."

"Let's forget the whole thing," Howie whispered. "We'll never be able to sneak past her."

"She's singing so loud, she'll never hear me. Just watch," Eddie said, pulling a big plastic bag from his backpack. Then he dropped to the floor and started crawling, holding the bag with his teeth. He crawled until he was right behind Mrs. Rosenbloom. Very slowly, Eddie stood up and dumped his anti-love potion into the big bowl of cookie dough. Eddie had just started mixing it when he felt something grab his cheek. It was a big hand with bright pink fingernails.

"Happy Valentine's Day, little boy. Looks like you've been caught with your hand in the cookie jar!" Mrs. Rosenbloom said, still holding on to Eddie's cheek.

Eddie's face turned as red as Mrs. Rosenbloom's lipstick. "I . . . I . . . I just wanted to taste one of your famous cookies. Everybody says they're delicious."

Mrs. Rosenbloom smiled and let go of Eddie's cheek. "Why, thanks for the compliment, honey."

"But I understand if you don't have any made yet," Eddie said quickly. "I'll just have to wait."

"Don't be silly." Mrs. Rosenbloom grabbed Eddie's arm and pulled him across the kitchen. "I happen to have one left from yesterday. I only give these to good friends, but you look pretty special to me."

Mrs. Rosenbloom held up a large red cookie. It was covered with globs of red sugar crystals. "Don't be shy," she said. "You can eat it."

Eddie opened his mouth to say, "No, thank you." But he didn't get a chance. As soon as he opened his mouth, Mrs. Rosenbloom stuck the cookie in.

"Yum!" Eddie said, with his mouth full. "This is delicious!" While Eddie was busy chomping on the cookie, Mrs. Rosenbloom quickly put a heart button onto his shirt.

"You're all ready for Valentine's Day," Mrs. Rosenbloom said. "Run along now."

Eddie met Howie back out in the hall. "Did you have to eat a cookie?" Howie squealed.

"I didn't have a choice," Eddie complained. "Besides, I'm too tough for a love potion to work on me."

"I hope you're right," Howie said, "because here comes Carey."

11

Head Over Heels

"Wow!" Eddie whispered. "Look how Carey's hair bounces!"

Howie grinned. "If it bounced any more, we could use her head for a basketball."

"And it's so shiny," Eddie continued as if he hadn't heard a word Howie said. "I just *love* it."

Howie stopped and stared at his best friend. "What did you say?"

"I just noticed how nice Carey looks, that's all," Eddie said.

Eddie smiled at Carey and Carey smiled back. She was looking at Eddie and didn't watch where she was going. *Wham!* Carey walked right into Ben, the meanest, toughest bully in the entire fourth grade.

They both fell, scattering books and homework all over the floor.

"I'd better help. Ben's liable to beat her up." Eddie rushed over to Carey and helped her up. Then he scrambled to pick up her things.

"Sorry," Ben apologized. "I didn't mean to run into you."

"What's got into him?" Eddie asked as Ben walked away. "He's usually so mean."

Carey shrugged her shoulders. Then she batted her eyelashes at Eddie. "'It was because you were protecting me. You probably saved my life."

Eddie stood up straight. "It was nothing. I'd be honored to carry your things to class," he said in his best grown-up voice.

"Pssst! We have a mission to complete," Howie called from across the hall.

"Can't you see I'm busy?" Eddie snapped. "Carey needs my help."

"But what about our plan?"

"What plan?" Carey asked sweetly.

Eddie smiled at her. "Howie and I were doing a little cooking, but I don't want to anymore."

"What about Mrs. Rosenbloom's cookies?" Howie said.

"Mmmm." Carey patted her stomach. "Those are the best cookies I've ever tasted."

"Maybe you should try one," Eddie told Howie. Then Eddie walked Carey into the classroom.

Howie slumped against the wall. "He's head over heels for Carey. Now what am I going to do?"

"It looks like you need some sweetening up," a voice echoed in the hall.

Howie jumped to see Mrs. Rosenbloom staring at him. "I don't need anything," he said.

"Now, sweetie, you're as sour as lemon peels. One of my special cookies will put a smile on your face."

"N-n-no thanks," Howie stammered and backed around a corner. He ran right into Liza and Melody.

"We've been looking all over for you," Melody said. "Have you decided yet?"

"Decided what?" Howie asked.

"Which one of us you like better, silly." Liza giggled.

Howie glared at the girls. "I'm beginning to think I don't like either of you."

Liza sniffed. "How dare you even think that!"

"I'm sorry," Howie said. "I didn't mean it."

"Well," Melody said loudly and crossed her arms. "You're going to have to decide and that's all there is to it." Liza crossed her arms and tapped her foot on the floor. Both girls stared at Howie.

"I . . . I . . ." Howie began.

"Yes?" Melody and Liza leaned close to Howie.

Howie took a deep breath. There was

only one thing to say. "I will make my decision right after lunch."

Both girls walked into the classroom whispering, "I bet he likes me better."

Howie gulped. He knew he wouldn't feel much like eating lunch today. He hoped that Mrs. Rosenbloom hadn't seen Eddie throw the anti-love potion into her cookie batter. It was his only chance. As a matter of fact, it was the only chance for Bailey Elementary.

12

Puppy Dog Tails

By lunchtime, Howie was feeling sick. He walked by himself to the lunchroom. Everyone else was blowing kisses and making goo-goo eyes at each other.

Filing through the lunch line, Howie caught a glimpse of Mrs. Rosenbloom's newest batch of cookies. There was a huge heart-shaped tray piled high with them. But today the cookies weren't bright red, they were sort of brown and splotchy.

"Yes!" Howie said to himself. The anti-love potion was in there, but would it work?

Mrs. Rosenbloom shook her head. "I'm not sure what happened. I followed my usual recipe, but today they look different. And for some reason there's enough

for the entire school. Help yourself."

Kids grabbed handfuls of the cookies and the pile dwindled away. Howie took his tray to a table in the corner of the cafeteria. He picked at his heart-shaped potato cake and looked around the room.

Eddie was giggling with Carey at a table in another corner. Liza and Melody were winking at him. Ben and Issy were staring into each other's eyes. Even Mrs. Jeepers was giving half her sugar cookie to Principal Davis.

Howie held his breath. People were eating the cookies!

"Yuck!" Principal Davis bellowed, spitting cookie everywhere. "This is the worst cookie I've ever tasted! What's in them?"

Puppy dog tails, Howie chuckled to himself.

Mrs. Rosenbloom rushed out of the kitchen as kids all over the cafeteria complained about the cookies. "What's wrong?" she asked.

"These cookies are horrible," Principal Davis told her.

Mrs. Rosenbloom shook her head and rushed back into the kitchen. "I don't understand. I didn't change the recipe one bit."

The next day at lunchtime, Liza and Melody brought their lunch trays over to sit with Howie.

"There's not a trace of yesterday's valentines," Melody said.

"This place looks so ordinary now," Liza said sadly. "I liked all the decorations." The three kids looked around the cafeteria. Not a single red or pink heart remained anywhere.

"I guess Mrs. Rosenbloom took them with her," Melody said. "I heard Principal Davis telling the secretary that she was moving to the mountains. She wanted to be up near the clouds on the mountaintop," he said.

"I guess we're free from Cupid's spells now." Howie sighed.

"Until next Valentine's Day," Liza added.

Eddie brought his tray and sat down beside them. "I fixed Carey." He giggled. "When she wasn't looking, I put pepper in her milk."

"I thought you liked Carey," Howie said.

Eddie rolled his eyes. "Are you crazy? I can't stand her."

Howie looked at Melody and Liza. "Are you guys still mad at each other?" he asked.

"What are you talking about? We never fight," Melody said.

"So we're still friends?" Howie asked hopefully, glad that things were getting back to normal.

"Of course," Melody and Liza said together. "We *love* being your friends."